After-School Monster

Marissa Moss

PUFFIN BOOKS

PUFFIN BOOKS
Published by the Penguin Group   Penguin Books USA Inc., 375 Hudson Street, New York, New York 10014, U.S.A.
Penguin Books Ltd, Registered Offices: Harmondsworth, Middlesex, England

First published in the United States of America by Lothrop, Lee, and Shepard Books, a division of William Morrow & Company, Inc., 1991
Reprinted by arrangement with William Morrow & Company, Inc.   Published in Puffin Books, 1993

1 3 5 7 9 10 8 6 4 2

LIBRARY OF CONGRESS CATALOGING-IN-PUBLICATION DATA
Moss, Marissa.   After-school monster / Marissa Moss.   p.   cm.   Summary: A little girl comes home after school and finds a monster in the house.
ISBN 0-14-054829-7   [1. Monsters—Fiction.] I. Title.   PZ7.M8535Af   1993   [E]—dc20   92-44488   CIP   AC
Printed in the United States of America

Luisa came home from school like she did every day. Her house looked peaceful and quiet. But when Luisa opened the door…

she stood toe to toe with a Monster.

"I'm going to gnash you! I'm going to bash you! I'm going to crash you!" said the Monster.

"Help!" said Luisa.

"Keep still!" shrieked the Monster. "I'm going to crunch, to munch, to eat you for my lunch!"

"No eating children allowed!" yelled
Luisa. "That's against the rules, and you'd
better follow them."

"Monsters don't follow rules. They break them," roared the Monster. "Now come here! You're my sweet, my treat, my morsel good to eat."

"Wait!" Luisa shouted. "Go next door to the Kapinskys' house. Twins live there. You'll have twice as much to eat."

"Phooey-kapooey-balooey," said the Monster. "The Kapinskys have their own monster. I'm *your* monster. You're the only one for me."

"Go away!" cried Luisa.

"Little girls don't tell monsters what to do. I'm bigger than you, and I'm stronger than you. I'm going to pluck you like a rose. I'm going to chew off your nose. I'm going to gobble up your toes." The Monster slurped.

"NOOOOO!" Luisa stomped her foot. "You won't! I'm strong too! Strong inside, where you can't get me!"

"Help," said the Monster.

"If the Kapinskys have their monster, and I have my monster, then *you* have *your* monster, and I'm it!" shouted Luisa.

"Help," whispered the Monster.

"I'm going to stomp you, to tromp you, to walla-walla-whomp you," Luisa growled.

"Help," mouthed the Monster.

"I'm going to flip you like a penny.
I'm going to crumble you like a cracker.
I'm going to throw you away like a rotten
banana peel," said Luisa calmly.

And she did.

Then Luisa cleaned up the house. She was finishing her homework when her mother got home.

"Did you have a good day, dear?" her mother asked.

"Uh-huh." Luisa smiled.

And the Monster went out with the garbage.